This book is for Nicholas and Norinda
~A M

For my godson Liam
~A E

Copyright © 2010 by Good Books, Intercourse, PA 17534

International Standard Book Number: 978-1-56148-683-0

Library of Congress Catalog Card Number: 2009033696

Text copyright © Angela McAllister 2010
Illustrations copyright © Alison Edgson 2010
Original edition published in English by Little Tiger Press,
an imprint of Magi Publications, London, England, 2010.
Printed in Singapore

Library of Congress Cataloging-in-Publication Data
McAllister, Angela.
Yuck! That's not a monster! / Angela McAllister ; illustrated by Alison Edgson.
p. cm. Summary: As Mr. and Mrs. Monster's three eggs begin to hatch, they
happily welcome the first two ugly little monsters to come out, but are shocked
and disappointed when they see what pops out of their last egg.
ISBN: 978-1-56148-683-0 (hardcover : alk. paper)
[1. Monsters--Fiction. 2. Parent and child--Fiction. 3. Individuality--Fiction.]
I. Edgson, Alison, ill. II. Title. III. Title: Yuck! That's not a monster!
PZ7.M47825Yu 2010 · [E]--dc22
2009033696

YUCK!
That's not a Monster!

Angela McAllister · Alison Edgson

Good Books

Intercourse, PA 17534
800/762-7171
www.GoodBooks.com

Mr. and Mrs. Monster were very
proud of their three eggs.
Mr. Monster kept them warm by
huffing with his hot, stinky breath.
Mrs. Monster screeched to them.

One stormy night,
the first egg cracked.
Out climbed an ugly
little monster with
prickly spikes and
snarly fangs.
"Aaah! He's FRIGHTFUL!"
sighed Mr. and Mrs.
Monster happily. So that's
what they called him.

Then the second egg cracked.
Out climbed another
ugly little monster
with horny spines and
bristly warts.
"Oooh! She's HORRID!"
gasped Mr. and Mrs. Monster
happily. So that's what
they called her.

Then the third egg shook a bit. Frightful
and Horrid gave it a poke. Out crept
something very soft and pink.
"UGH! HE'S SWEET!!"
said the little monsters.
"LET'S SQUASH HIM!"

"Well, he's not what we expected," said Mrs. Monster. "He is a bit of a shock."

"Let's throw him in the trash can," said Mr. Monster.

Suddenly there was a crash of thunder.

"*Mama!*" cried the fluffy one and jumped into Mrs. Monster's arms. She looked down at her bundle of sweetness. "I think we'll keep him," she said. "He may look different but inside he is a monster, just like us."

So they called him Little Shock.

Each day Frightful and Horrid grew hairier and scarier.

They learned how to spit and hiss and snarl and scratch.

But Little Shock grew MORE
fluffy. He liked to gurgle and roly-poly
and twinkle his big blue eyes. He loved
his brother and sister and followed
them everywhere.

Awoooooooooooo!

"If you want to play with us, you need to be wild and rambunctious," said Frightful and Horrid. They showed him how to howl at the moon until it hid behind a cloud. But Little Shock was afraid of the dark.

They showed him how to squash and stomp and trample. But Little Shock saw a worried worm and sat down to give it a hug.

"Ugh!" sneered Frightful and Horrid. "He's just a cutie-pie!"

Soon Frightful and Horrid were bold enough to go monstering in the woods.

"You must take your brother with you," insisted Mrs. Monster.

Frightful and Horrid snorted grumpily but they put Little Shock in a wagon, hid him under a blanket and tugged him along.

In the woods, Frightful leaped out at a fox and made its fur turn white. Horrid pounced on a wild pig and made it jump into a tree. They had a wonderful time!

GRRR!

RARGH!

Little Shock hugged his blanket
and played peek-a-boo with a mouse.

"What shall we do now?"
said Frightful.
"Let's find something big
to scare," said Horrid.
Something big rustled in the
bushes ahead, so they crept up on it.
Frightful and Horrid saw a hairy hump.
They winked at each other, took
a deep breath and . . . .

ROARED!

But the hairy hump was only a little bit of a BIG monster! It snarled and flashed its fiery eyes. "WHO DARED TO ROAR AT ME?"

Frightful and Horrid were
too terrified to run away.
Their spines shriveled and
their claws curled up.

Suddenly the BIG monster
spotted Little Shock.
"OOOH! COTTON CANDY!"
he said.

Little Shock stared up at the
monster's face. His big blue eyes
grew wider and wider . . .

Then **MWAH!**
He gave the monster
a kiss right on
the cheek!

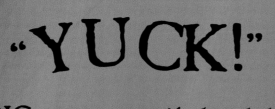

"YUCK!"

The BIG monster wailed and dropped Little
Shock in horror. He was so afraid that his fur
turned to frizz and his bristles fell out.

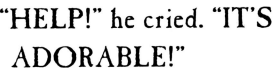

"HELP!" he cried. "IT'S ADORABLE!"
     And he ran away, crying for his mommy.

Frightful and Horrid couldn't believe their eyes.
     "You kissed him! You kissed him!" they laughed.

Horrid swung her little brother high in the air
and sat him on Frightful's shoulders.
"Maybe being cute is useful after all,"
she said, giving him a pinch.
Little Shock just purred happily.
"Come on," said Frightful proudly.
"Let's go home and ALL kiss Mom and Dad!"

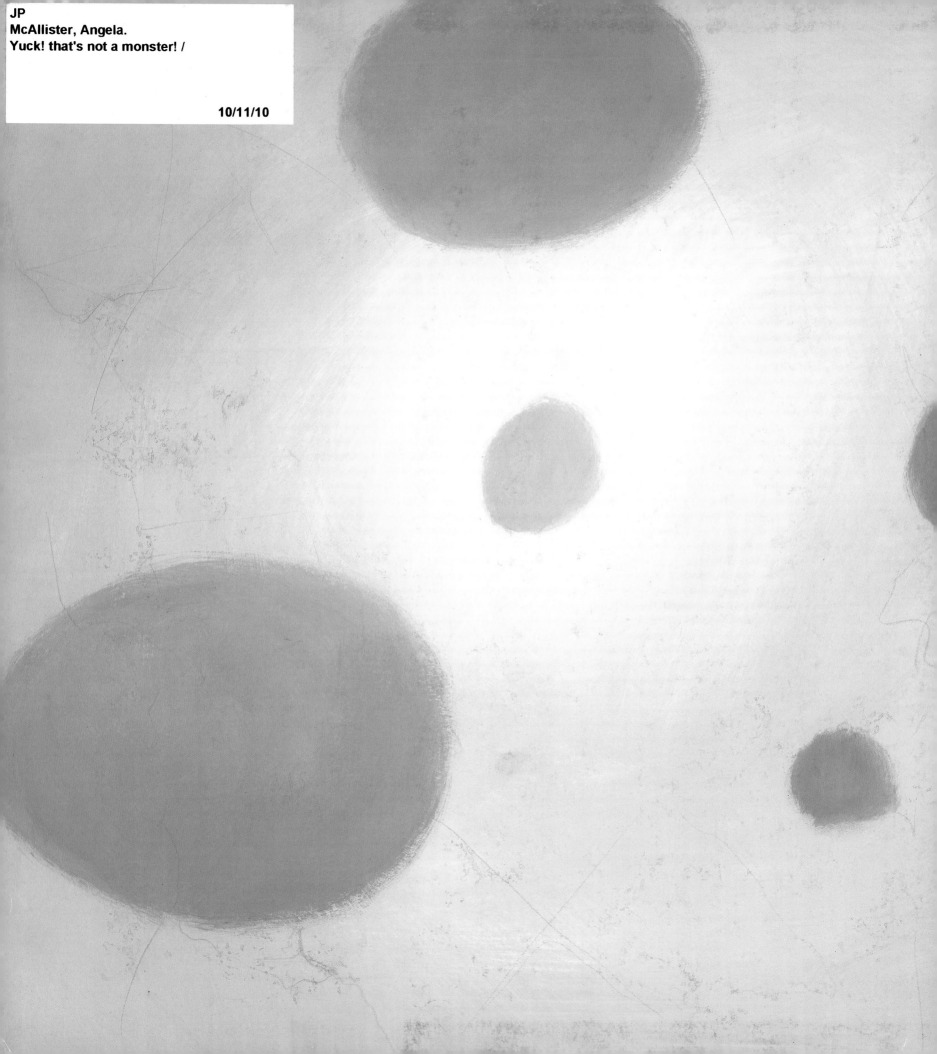